Headlamp

Radio

Firefighters

Fire Chief

CEDAR MILL
P9-CLS-310
WITHDRAWN
CEDAR MILL LIBRARY

Flashlights

Boots

Ax

Pike Pole

Air Mask

Air Tank

Ladder Truck

For Hobey, an armful of warm boy
—M. C.

For Nora & Lena
—B. K.

**Thanks to the heroic firefighters at the Trenton Fire Headquarters
in Trenton, NJ, for offering helpful feedback on the text and artwork.**

Henry Holt and Company
Publishers since 1866
175 Fifth Avenue, New York, New York 10010
mackids.com

Henry Holt® is a registered trademark of Macmillan Publishing Group, LLC.
Text copyright © 2017 by Margery Cuyler
Illustrations copyright © 2017 by Bob Kolar
All rights reserved.

Library of Congress Cataloging-in-Publication Data is available.
ISBN 978-1-62779-805-1

Our books may be purchased in bulk for promotional, educational, or
business use. Please contact your local bookseller or the Macmillan Corporate
and Premium Sales Department at (800) 221-7945 ext. 5442 or by e-mail at
MacmillanSpecialMarkets@macmillan.com.

First Edition—2017
The artist used Adobe Illustrator on a Macintosh computer to
create the illustrations for this book.

Printed in China by RR Donnelley Asia Printing Solutions Ltd.,
Dongguan City, Guangdong Province
1 3 5 7 9 10 8 6 4 2

The Little Fire Truck

Margery Cuyler

illustrated by Bob Kolar

Christy Ottaviano Books

Henry Holt and Company • New York

I'm a little fire truck,
my driver's name is Jill.
We zip all over town,
my siren's loud and shrill.

I'm a little fire truck,
there's lots of work to do.
We put out smoky fires
and rescue animals, too.

I'm a little fire truck,
I'm engine forty-five.
Big lights flash! Time to dash!
A fire's on Lake Drive.

I'm a little fire truck,
the crew slides down the pole.
Firefighters hurry;
each has a special role.

I'm a little fire truck—
they jump into their boots,
grab their masks and helmets,
headlamps, tanks, and suits.

I'm a little fire truck,
my air horn starts to blast.
BLAM! BLAM! BLAM! BLAAA-AAAAM!
We leave the station fast.

I'm a little fire truck,
Jill's pumping water out.
Splish-splosh! Splish-splosh! Splish-splosh!
It's flowing through my spout.

I'm a little fire truck,
tall ladders reach so high.
Firefighters climbing
as smoke fills up the sky.

I'm a little fire truck,
the crew breaks down the doors.
Holding pikes and axes,
they crawl along the floors.

I'm a little fire truck,
the chief and captain shout,
"No one's home, no one's hurt,
the fire's finally out."

I'm a little fire truck,
Jill drives our fighters back.
They check and clean their gear,
hang hoses on the rack.

I'm a little fire truck,
we work hard night and day,
speeding to the rescue,
I love my job—HOORAY!

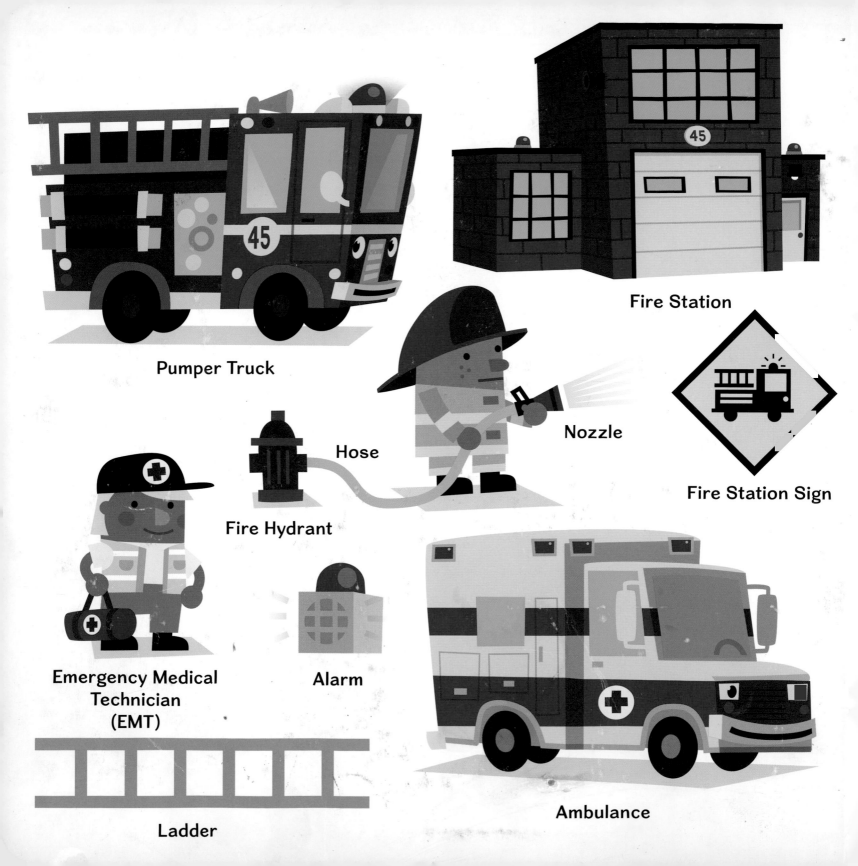

Pumper Truck

Fire Station

Nozzle

Fire Station Sign

Hose

Fire Hydrant

Emergency Medical
Technician
(EMT)

Alarm

Ambulance

Ladder